WHO WILL PICK ME UP WHEN I FALL?

Dorothy E. Molnar and Stephan H. Fenton

Illustrated by Irene Trivas

ALBERT WHITMAN & COMPANY, Morton Grove, Illinois

The illustrations are watercolor and pencil.
The text typeface is ITC Benguiat Gothic Medium.

Library of Congress Cataloging-in-Publication Data

Molnar, Dorothy E.
   Who will pick me up when I fall? /
Dorothy E. Molnar and Stephan H. Fenton ;
pictures by Irene Trivas.
        p. cm.
   Summary: A young child with a working mother, who
spends each day after school with someone else, needs
Mommy's reassurance of love.
   ISBN 0-8075-9072-X (lib. bdg.)
   [1. Mothers and daughters—Fiction.   2. Working
mothers—Fiction.] I. Fenton, Stephan H.   II. Trivas,
Irene, ill.   III. Title.
PZ7.M7348Wh   1991   90-28250
[E]—dc20   CIP
                                                   AC

Text © 1991 by Dorothy E. Molnar and
Stephan H. Fenton.
Illustrations © 1991 by Irene Trivas.
Published in 1991 by Albert Whitman & Company,
6340 Oakton Street, Morton Grove, Illinois 60053-2723.
Published simultaneously in Canada
by General Publishing, Limited, Toronto.
All rights reserved. Printed in the U.S.A.
10 9 8 7 6 5 4 3 2 1

To our little Sarton, who each morning had to ask,
"Who will pick me up today?"   DEM SHF

My eyes open before
I'm awake. I jump out of
bed. I jump back in. I can't
remember what day it is.

With my chin on my knees,
I try to think. It's Monday if
Alexa's mom picks me up
after school and takes me to
the gym.

Or, is today Tuesday, the day José's daddy takes us swimming? He lets me jump off the diving board into the water that looks like broken glass.

Then Ann meets me. She
dries my hair with a smelly
yellow towel and walks me
home. She gives me three
crackers with peanut butter,
and we wait for Mommy.

Oh-oh, Mommy's calling me to get dressed. I *think* my teacher, Ms. Breton, told me that today I'd go with T.J. for dance lessons after school. So then it's Wednesday.

After dance lessons I go to
T.J.'s. He promised on his life
that this time I could try his
new two-wheeler. But who will
pick me up when I fall?

I guess I'll wear my purple leotard for dancing. But Mikey told me I was eating dinner at his house. He said we're having green spaghetti and prunes.

There is no day I go to Mikey's house. Hey, what day is this? Anyway, I hate prunes and I don't even like Mikey. He always burps at the lunch table.

I'm going to curl up under my blanket as quiet and smooth as an O. And Mommy will forget I'm here.

She'll rush out the door,
her briefcase latch hanging
dangling banging open. She'll
rush back in because she
forgot her keys.

She'll jump in the car,
knocking her knee, and say
a naughty word as she drives
away. Forgetting about
little O me.

Then I'll uncurl my O and jump out of bed. I'll play and play and play some more and not care what day it is. I won't have to think, "Who is picking me up after school?" I won't have to remember if I'm going to dancing, to swimming, to the dark, cavelike gym.

All day I'll be home, waiting for Mommy to come back.

Mommy's calling again—
"Are you dressed? Are your
teeth brushed? Do you need
a dime for milk?"
Shh, I just won't answer.

Mommy's found me.
She's scolding me—
"How come you're not dressed?
How come you're not washed?
How come your red pack isn't
packed? Oh, Sarton, Sarton,
you're going to make us late."

"I'm not going to school,"
I mumble. Mommy asks me
what I said.

"Nothing," I say. But I slide
out of bed and pull on my blue
overalls, the ones with the
loud snaps. Mommy rushes to
the kitchen, calling back that
I'm a good girl. I whisper to
myself, "If I'm so good, how
come you don't want to be
with me?"

Should I pack my swimsuit
or my purple leotard or my
overdue book for the library?
I spin around and around like a
top until the sky is swallowed
gently by the ground.

What day is it, anyway?

I go downstairs and from under the sink I take six big brown bags. Then I run back to my room. In the Monday bag, I pack my black gym sneakers and my lucky rock. In the Tuesday bag, my swimsuit and a towel. In the Wednesday bag, my leotard and dancing shoes. In the Thursday bag, my sweaty soccer shirt.

As I'm packing the Friday bag Mommy comes in. She sees the brown bags lined up like traffic.

"What are you doing, Sarton?" she says. I tell her.

"What will you pack in the last bag, sweetie?" she asks.

"My red sweater, a flashlight, my Lambie, bubble gum, and a picture of you."

"Why?" Mommy asks.
"In case," I answer.
"In case what?"
"In case I run away."
"Why would you run away?"
she wants to know.
"When I can't remember
what day it is, or where I'm
supposed to go, or who's
taking me there. On that day,
I'll grab the no-day bag and go.
But not too far."

Suddenly Mommy kneels
down. She hugs me hard.

Then she runs into her room
and comes back carrying her
reindeer sweater with the big
pockets and a fat book.

"Here, Sarton, put these in
the no-day bag," she says.

"Why, Mommy?"
"In case," she answers.
"In case what, Mommy?"
"In case I run away with you." Her voice sounds like when she whispered goodbye on my first day of school.
"Then I won't need your picture," I say. We both laugh.

"On Friday," Mommy says, "I'll take off from work and we'll spend the whole day together. And you know what?"

"What?" I say.

"You can do whatever you like."

"Eat ice cream for breakfast, wear my jeans with the torn knees, and visit the hippo at the zoo?"

"Yes. Now hurry up or we'll both be late," Mommy calls as she runs for her coat.

How will I know which day
is Friday, I wonder. Just to be
safe, I pack Mommy's sweater
and fat book in the no-day bag
and push it under my bed.

Mommy shouts that Sasha's mom is beeping her horn for me. Oh, it's WEDNESDAY!

I grab my leotard and
dancing shoes and run out
the door!